Contents

KU-247-091

The Three Dogs 4
By the Brothers Grimm

The Princess and the Hare 12
A traditional German tale

Earl Mar's Daughter 22
By Joseph Jacobs

The Sea-Hare 31
By the Brothers Grimm

The Three Dogs

By the Brothers Grimm

THERE WAS ONCE a shepherd who had a son and a daughter. On his deathbed he said, "I have nothing to leave you but three sheep and a house — divide them between you, as you like." The brother asked his sister which she would like best, and she chose the house. "Then I'll take the sheep and go out to seek my fortune," he said.

One day on his travels, he met a man with three dogs, at a crossroad.

"Hello, my fine fellow," said the man,

"I see you have three sheep. If you'll give them to me, I'll give you my three dogs."

The youth smiled and replied, "What would I do with your dogs?"

"My dogs are not like other dogs," said the stranger. "The smallest one is called Salt. He will bring you food whenever you wish. The second dog is called Pepper, and he will tear anyone who tries to hurt you to pieces. The third and biggest one is called Mustard, and he is so powerful that he can break iron with his teeth."

The shepherd happily gave the stranger his sheep in return for the dogs. Every day Salt brought him a fine meal and he went along merrily.

One day he met a carriage, all draped in black. Inside sat a beautiful girl, crying. The

coachman told him that a dragon lived nearby, and every year it ate a maiden. This year its choice had fallen on the king's daughter. The shepherd felt sad and decided to follow the carriage.

After a while the carriage stopped and the girl got out. When she had walked halfway up the hill, a terrible monster with the body of a snake, and with huge wings and claws, came towards her. The shepherd called, "Pepper, come to the rescue," and

the second dog set
upon the dragon.

After a fierce struggle Pepper
conquered the monster, and ate it
all up – except for its two front teeth,
which the shepherd picked up and
put in his pocket.

The princess begged the shepherd to return with her to her father, who would reward him richly. But the youth said that he wanted to see something of the world, and that he would return again in three years' time. So, bidding each other farewell, she and the shepherd separated.

But while the princess was driving home the carriage suddenly stood still, and the coachman turned to her and said, "You must tell your father that it was I who killed the dragon, or I will throw you into the river, and no one will be any the wiser, for they will think the dragon has devoured you."

The princess was in a dreadful state when she heard these words, but there was nothing she could do but to promise. They returned to the capital, and everyone was delighted when they saw the princess. The king hugged his daughter with tears of joy, and turning to the coachman said, "You have saved the life of my precious child, you shall be rewarded. Take her for your wife, but as she is still so young, do not let the wedding happen for another year."

The poor princess wept bitterly, but she could not break her promise. When the year was over, she begged hard for another.

When this year passed also, she begged so hard for one more year that the king's heart melted, and he agreed, much to the princess's joy, for she knew that her real rescuer would soon appear.

And so the year passed away, and the wedding day was fixed, and all the people were prepared to make merry and feast.

On the wedding day the shepherd returned with his three dogs. He asked what was the meaning of all the feasting and celebration, and they told him that the king's daughter was going to be married to the man who had killed the dragon. The shepherd at once announced that the coachman was a liar, but no one would listen to him, and he was thrown into a dungeon for causing trouble on the wedding day.

While he was lying there, planning how to escape, an idea dawned on him, and he called out, "Mustard, come to my help," and before he could count to two the creature had bitten through the iron bars and stood beside him. The king had just arrived at the church, when the shepherd appeared. The former coachman grew as white as a sheet when he saw the shepherd, and, falling on his knees, begged for mercy. The princess recognized her saviour at once, and did not need the proof of the dragon's teeth, which he drew from his pocket.

After seeing the teeth, the king was convinced that the shepherd was telling the truth. The coachman was thrown into the dungeon, and the shepherd took his rightful place with the princess. This time she did not ask for the wedding to be put off, and they all lived happily ever after together.

The Princess and the Hare

A traditional German tale

THERE WAS ONCE a queen who desperately wanted a child, so she went to the Sun and said, "Please send me a little girl, and when she is twelve years old you may take her back."

So the Sun sent her a little girl, and the queen named her Letiko. She cared for her until she was twelve years old. Soon after her birthday, while Letiko was gathering herbs, the Sun came to her and said, "Remind your mother of her promise."

When the queen heard this she shut all the doors and windows of the palace and stopped up all the chinks and holes, so that the Sun should not take Letiko away. But she forgot to close up the keyhole, and through it the Sun sent a ray into the house,

/

which took hold of the little girl and carried her away to him. And there she lived with the Sun and did his work.

One day, the Sun sent Letiko to fetch some straw. She sat down on the piles of straw and said, "As sighs this straw under my feet so sighs my heart for my mother."

This caused her to be so long away that the Sun asked her, when she came back, "Why have you been so long?"

She answered, "My slippers are too big, and I could not go faster."

So the Sun made the slippers smaller.

Another time he sent her to fetch water. At the spring she sat down and said, "As flows the water so flows my heart with longing for my mother."

She remained so long away that the Sun asked her why. She answered, "My petticoat is too long and hinders me in walking."

So the Sun cut her petticoat shorter.

Another time, the Sun sent her to bring him a pair of sandals, and as the princess carried these in her hand she said, "As creaks the leather so creaks my heart after my mother."

When she came home the Sun asked again, "Why do you come home so late?"

"My red hood is too wide, and it falls over my eyes."

Then he made the hood narrower.

At last, however, the Sun realized how sad Letiko was. He sent her a second time to bring straw, and, slipping in after her, he heard how she cried for her mother.

So, being not really bad-hearted, he went home, called two foxes to him, and said, "If you were to take Princess Letiko home what would you eat and drink if you should become hungry and thirsty?"

"Why, we would eat her flesh and drink her blood."

When the Sun heard that, he told the foxes that they were not suitable. So he sent them away, and called two hares to him, and said, "If you were to take Princess Letiko home what would you eat and drink if you should become hungry and thirsty on your journey?"

"We will eat grass and drink from streams, of course."

"You may take her home," said the Sun.

So he said goodbye to Letiko and the hares set out with the princess. After a time they became hungry, so they said to the little girl, "Climb this tree, and stay there till we have finished eating some grass."

So Letiko climbed the tree, and the hares went grazing on grass.

While they were eating, an evil snake-woman came to the tree and said, "Letiko, come down and see what beautiful shoes I have on. If you will not come down I'll cut down the tree and eat you all up."

"Just try to cut down it down," said Letiko,

calmly, "and then eat me."

So the snake-woman chopped with all her strength but no matter how hard she tried, she could not cut the tree down. When she realized, she called up to Letiko, "Come down, I must feed my children."

"Go home and feed them then, and come back when you are ready," said Letiko.

When the snake-woman had gone enough far away, Princess Letiko called out loudly, "Little hares! Little hares! Please come back here!"

They both ran back to her as fast as their little legs could go. Then Letiko came down from the tree, and they quickly went on their way. But soon the snake-woman was hurrying back to find them.

As Letiko drew near to the palace, the queen's dog recognized her, and called out happily, "Bow wow! Bow wow! Here is Letiko! My Queen, she is coming back to the palace at last!"

But the sad queen said, "Hush! Will you make me burst with misery? I miss Letiko so much it breaks my heart! I wish she could return home to me."

Next the queen's cat, which was lazing on the roof, saw her and called out, "Miaow! Miaow! Here comes Letiko! She is coming home to the palace."

The queen sobbed, "Please, keep silent! The Sun has my dear Letiko now, and I shall never see her again."

Soon Letiko and the two hares were very near the palace, but so too was the snake-woman. As they reached the back door of the palace the hares hustled Letiko inside. The first hare ran in with her, but just as the second hare was about to slip in too, the snake-woman caught it by its little tail and tore it off!

As the second hare came in, the queen stood up and said, "Welcome, dear little hare. Because you

have brought back my daughter Letiko I will give you a beautiful silver tail."

And she did so, and lived happily ever after with her daughter, Princess Letiko.

Earl Mar's Daughter

By Joseph Jacobs

ONE FINE SUMMER'S DAY, Earl Mar's daughter went into the castle grounds. As she strolled through the gardens she would stop from time to time to listen to the music of the birds. After a while she rested, and sat in the shade of a green oak tree. She looked up and saw a dove sitting high up on one of its branches. Earl Mar's daughter said to the bird, "Coo-my-dove, my dear, come down to me and I will give you a golden cage. I'll take you home and look after you well."

As she said these words the dove flew down from the branch and settled on her shoulder, nestling up against her neck while she smoothed its feathers. Then she took it home to her room.

The day was nearly over, and Earl Mar's daughter was thinking of going to sleep when, as she turned around, she found at her side a handsome young man. She was startled, for the door had been locked for hours. But she was a brave girl and so

23

she said, "What are you doing here?"

"Hush! Hush!" the young man whispered. "I was the cooing dove that you coaxed down from the tree."

"But who are you?" she said quietly, "and how did you come to be changed into that dear little bird?"

"My name is Florentine, and my mother is a queen — something more than a queen actually — for she knows magic. I would not do as she wished, so she turned me into a dove by day, but at night her spells lose their power and I become a man again. Today I crossed the sea and saw you for the first time. I was glad to be a bird, so that I could come near you. Unless you love me, I'll never be happy."

"But if I love you," said she, "will you not fly away and leave me one day?"

"Never, never," said the prince "be my wife and I'll be yours forever. By day a bird, by night a prince, I will always be by your side as a husband, dear."

Somehow the girl knew that it was the right thing to do — she had fallen in love with the young man at first sight. They were married in secret and lived happily in the castle and no one knew that every night Coo-my-dove became Prince Florentine.

Seven years passed and then a great trouble came to them. Earl Mar wished to marry his daughter to a fine man who came wooing her. Her father insisted but she said, "Father, I do not wish to marry, I can be quite happy with Coo-my-dove here."

Then her father flew into a mighty rage and said, "Tomorrow, so sure as I live, I'll twist that bird's neck," and he stamped out

of her room in a rage.

"Oh no!" said Coo-my-dove, "It's time that I left," and in a moment he was flying away. And he flew and he flew over the deep, deep sea, till he came to his mother's castle.

The queen, his mother, was taking a walk when she saw the pretty dove flying overhead and alighting on the castle walls.

"Here dancers, come and dance your jigs," she called, "and pipers, pipe you well, for here's my own Florentine, come back to me to stay."

"No, mother," said Florentine, "no dancers for me and no minstrels, for my dear wife is to be wed tomorrow, it is a sad day for me."

"What can I do, my son?" said the queen, "tell me, and it shall be done if my magic has the power to do it."

"Please turn the twenty-four dancers into twenty-four grey herons, and let my pipers become seven white swans, and let me be a goshawk and their leader."

"Alas my son," she said, "my magic is not strong enough for that. But perhaps the witch-wife of Ostree may be able to help. I shall go and see her straight away."

And away she hurried to the witch-wife's cave to speak to her. After a while the queen came out, muttering over some burning herbs. Suddenly Coo-my-dove changed into a goshawk and around him flew twenty-four grey herons and above them flew seven swans.

Without a word or a goodbye off they flew over the deep blue sea. They flew and they flew until they swooped down on Earl Mar's castle just as the wedding party were setting out for the church.

First came the men-at-arms and then the bridegroom's friends. Then came Earl Mar's men, followed by the bridegroom. And lastly, pale and beautiful, Earl Mar's daughter herself. They moved slowly until they came past the trees on which the birds were settling. Prince Florentine, the goshawk, gave the word and they all rose into the air. The wedding guests wondered at the sight when, swoop! The herons were down among them scattering the crowd.

The swans took the bride while the goshawk dashed down and tied the bridegroom to a tree. Then the herons

gathered themselves into one feather bed.
The swans placed the princess upon them,
and suddenly they all rose in the air bearing
the bride away with them in safety towards

Prince Florentine's home.

Surely a wedding party was never so disturbed in this world! What could they do? They watched the pretty bride be carried away until she and all the birds disappeared. That very day Prince Florentine brought Earl Mar's daughter to his mother's castle. She took the spell off him and they lived happily ever after.

The Sea-Hare

By the Brothers Grimm

NCE UPON A TIME, there was a beautiful princess who lived in a grand palace. The palace had a tall tower with twelve windows that looked out in every direction. When she gazed through them, she could inspect her whole kingdom.

When she looked out of the first window, she could see more than any other human being. From the second window she could see still better, and so it went on, until the

The Sea-Hare

twelfth window, from which she saw everything above the earth and under the earth. Nothing at all could be kept secret from her. She was proud, and didn't want to share her kingdom, so she declared that no one would ever be her husband unless he could hide himself where she couldn't find him. Anyone who tried this and was found would be put in prison.

Ninety-seven men were already imprisoned in dungeons below the castle, and no one had come forward for a long time. The princess was delighted, and thought to herself, 'Now I shall be free as long as I live.'

Then three brothers came before her, and said that they wanted to try their luck. The eldest crept into a deep pit, but the princess saw him from the first window, made him come out and put him in prison. The second hid in the cellar of the palace, but she saw him also, and his fate was sealed. Then the youngest came and begged her to let him have three tries. As he was so handsome, and she liked the look of him, she said yes.

The Sea-Hare

The youngest brother thought about how he should hide himself, but in vain. So he seized his bow and arrow and went out hunting. After a short time he saw a raven, and was just going to fire, when the bird cried out to him, " Please don't shoot me — I will make it worth your while."

So the youth put his bow down and went on. He soon came to a lake and sat down to rest. As he watched the water a fish came up to the surface. The youngest brother took out his bow and arrow once more and took aim. The fish cried, "Stop! If you don't attack me I will reward you."

The youngest brother allowed the fish to dive down again and went onwards. He soon met a fox.

He wanted to kill the fox and skin it, but the fox said, "Stop, and I will make it worth your while." The youth let it go, then decided to return home.

The next day the youngest brother was meant to hide himself, but he could not think where, so he went into the forest to the raven and said, "Tell me where I can go to hide myself, so that the king's daughter shall not see me."

The raven thought it over for a long time.

Then it fetched an egg from its nest, cut it into two, and shut the youth inside it. The raven then made it whole again, and seated itself on it.

When the king's daughter went to the first window she could not see the young man, nor could she from the other windows. But from the eleventh window she saw the egg moving slightly. She ordered the raven to be captured and the egg to be brought and broken, and the youth came out.

"If you can't do better than that," said the princess, "you've lost the challenge!"

The next day the youth went to the lake, called the fish and begged it to help him. So the fish swallowed him, and went down to the bottom of the lake.

The king's daughter looked through her windows, and even from the eleventh she could not see him. She was worried, but at last from the twelfth window she saw the bulge in the fish's stomach.

She ordered the fish to be caught and squeezed, and then the youth appeared.

"Twice you are forgiven," said the princess, "but be sure — you will be locked up tomorrow."

On the last day, the young man went with a heavy heart, and met the fox.

"You are clever," said he, "where shall I hide myself so that the king's daughter cannot discover me?"

"That's very hard indeed," answered the fox, looking very thoughtful. But then it took the young man to a magic spring, dipped itself in it, and came out as a stall-keeper from the market. The youth then dipped himself in the water too, and

changed into a sea-hare, a sea creature similar to a large slug.

The stall-keeper went into the town, and many people came to see the sea-hare. The princess came too and bought it. Before the stall-keeper handed over the sea-hare to the princess he whispered to it, "When the princess goes to the window, creep under the braids of her hair." And so he did. The princess went from window to window but

The Sea-Hare

could not see the young man.
When she failed to spot
him from the twelfth
window, she was furious
at being beaten.
She felt the sea-hare
beneath her braids and
threw it out of the
window as far as she
could. The sea-hare
soon found the stall-
keeper and they both
hurried back to
the spring.
After they had
changed back to
their true forms
they parted ways.
The youth returned

to the princess and they were married, but he never told her where he had hidden himself for the third time, and who had helped him.

The princess believed that the youth had done everything by himself, and she had a great respect for him, and they lived happily ever after.